FRANKLIN PARK PUBLIC
3 1316 00367
W9-AWQ-118

THE HARDY BOYS®

UNDERCOVER BROTHERS™

PAPERCUTZ™

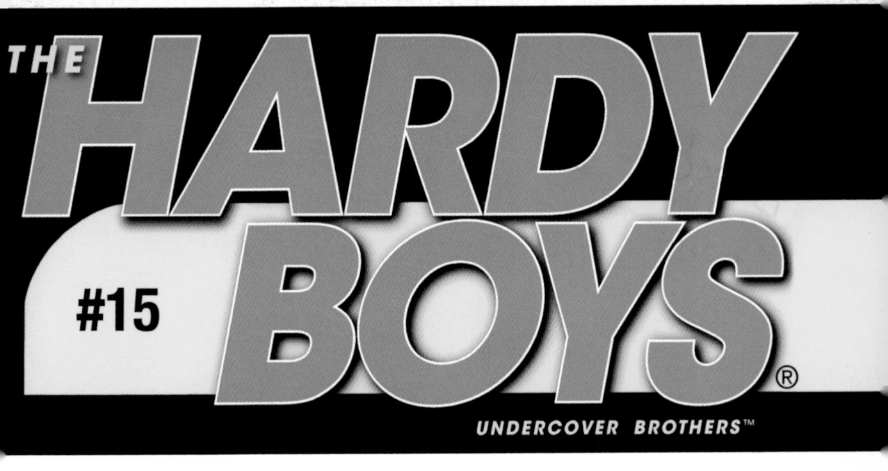

Live Free, Die Hardy!

SCOTT LOBDELL • Writer
PAULO HENRIQUE MARCONDES • Artist

Based on the series by
FRANKLIN W. DIXON

PAPERCUTZ™
New York

Live Free, Die Hardy!
SCOTT LOBDELL — Writer
PAULO HENRIQUE MARCONDES — Artist
MARK LERER — Letterer
LAURIE E. SMITH — Colorist
MIKHAELA REID & MASHEKA WOOD— Production
MICHAEL PETRANEK — Editorial Assistant
JIM SALICRUP
Editor-in-Chief

ISBN 10: 1-59707-123-4 paperback edition
ISBN 13: 978-1-59707-123-9 paperback edition
ISBN 10: 1-59707-124-2 hardcover edition
ISBN 13: 978-1-59707-124-6 hardcover edition

Published by arrangement with Aladdin Paperbacks,
an imprint of Simon & Schuster Children's Publishing Division.

Distributed by Macmillan.

Printed in China.

10 9 8 7 6 5 4 3 2 1

CHAPTER ONE: "BRAVEHARDY!"
MY NAME IS JOE HARDY.
I'M THE YOUNGER, BLONDER, MORE DASHING OF THE TWO.
MY WINGMAN AND BROTHER IS FRANK.
WE'VE HAD SOME PRETTY WILD CASES SINCE WE BECAME UNDER-COVER BROTHERS FOR A.T.A.C*...
...BUT THIS ONE IS THE CRAZIEST.
AWESOME, RIGHT?
*A.T.A.C.: AMERICAN TEENS AGAINST CRIME.

"DIFFERENT," YES.
"UNORTHODOX," DEFINITELY.
"AWESOME"? NOT SO MUCH, NO.

ADMIT IT--
YOU'RE HAVING
A BLAST!
YEAH, HE MIGHT
GROUSE SOME-
TIMES--
LIKE WHEN A SITUATION
VEERS A LITTLE TOO FAR
FROM NORMAL.
BUT IF YOU'RE EVER
SURROUNDED BY AN ARMY
OF MAGICAL WARRIORS...
TRUST ME--HE'S
THE GUY YOU WANT
AT YOUR BACK!

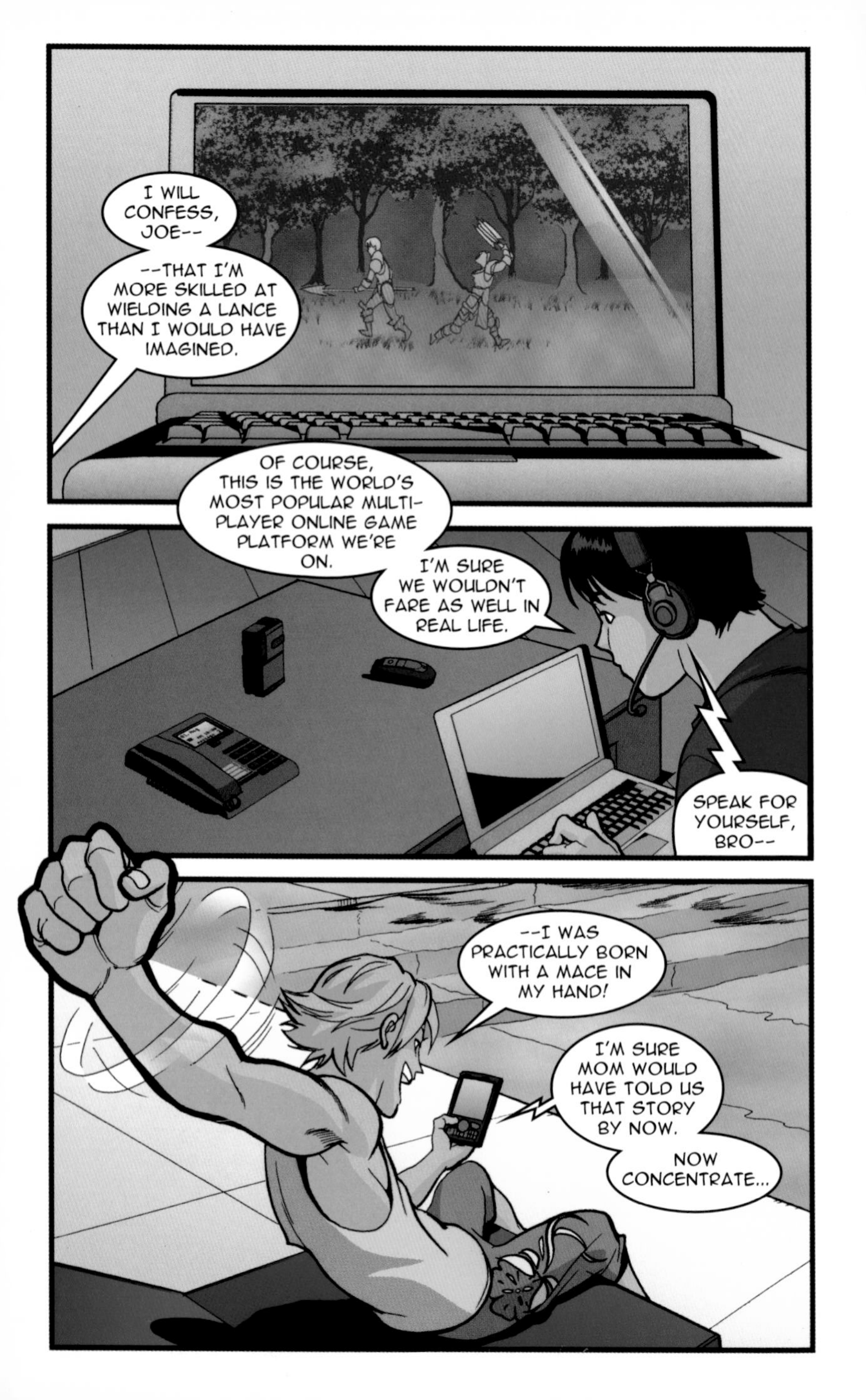
I WILL CONFESS, JOE--
--THAT I'M MORE SKILLED AT WIELDING A LANCE THAN I WOULD HAVE IMAGINED.
OF COURSE, THIS IS THE WORLD'S MOST POPULAR MULTI-PLAYER ONLINE GAME PLATFORM WE'RE ON.
I'M SURE WE WOULDN'T FARE AS WELL IN REAL LIFE.
SPEAK FOR YOURSELF, BRO--
--I WAS PRACTICALLY BORN WITH A MACE IN MY HAND!
I'M SURE MOM WOULD HAVE TOLD US THAT STORY BY NOW.
NOW CONCENTRATE...

A LOT OF PEOPLE THINK THE BIG DIFFERENCE BETWEEN US --
... WHILE I PROVIDE A DISTRACTION!
--IS I'M MORE THE ACTION GUY AND FRANK IS MORE THE BRAINIAC.
BUT THE TRUTH IS MY BROTHER EXCELS AT EVERYTHING.
?!
WHICH IS WHY I'M KIND OF IN AWE OF HIM.
ALLEY OOP!
REMEMBER WHAT WE TALKED ABOUT, JOE--
BUT I'D DENY IT IF HE ASKED.
I DON'T WANT HIS HEAD SWELL-ING UP SO BIG HE CAN'T PULL STUNTS LIKE THIS!

--WE'VE PLANNED THIS TO A "T."
HE'S BIG WITH PLANS.
IN THIS CASE, HE CAME UP WITH A GOOD ONE.
I'M ALL EYES, FRANK.
EXCEPT FOR THE HANDS I'M USING TO BEAT DOWN THESE DUDES.
THERE'S AN AVATAR HERE IN THE GAME (AN ICON THAT REPRESENTS A REAL-LIFE PLAYER)--
--WHO'S BEEN USING THIS MULTI-PLATFORM GAME TO INJECT VIRUSES INTO INNOCENT TEENAGERS' COMPUTERS.
BINGO.
THERE SHE IS!

SHE WAITS UNTIL THE HEAT OF BATTLE BEFORE SHE STRIKES.
SHE'S ALREADY TAKEN OUT DOZENS OF COM-PUTERS THROUGHOUT THE COUNTRY!

FRANK--DO YOU SEE HER?!
IF SHE FIRES THAT ARROW, ANOTHER COMPUTER SYSTEM BITES THE DUST!

THAT'S NOT GOING TO HAPPEN!
WHEN HE SAYS THINGS LIKE THAT--ALL DETERMINED--I BELIEVE HIM.
ALWAYS.

MR. PENHURST? NIGEL--ARE YOU THERE?
BLEEP!
WE'RE IN A ONE MILE RADIUS OF WHERE WE EXPECT TO FIND THE SUSPECT.
TRANSMITTING HER CYBER-ADDRESS...NOW!
WE'VE RECEIVED IT, FRANK!
THE A.T.A.C. COMPUTERS ARE HONING IN ON THE REAL WORLD ADDRESS NOW!
KEEP HER ONLINE ANOTHER MINUTE AND WE'LL BE KNOCKING ON HER FRONT DOOR
ONE MINUTE, HUH...?

...THAT'S EASY FOR YOU TO SAY!
WHAT ARE YOU TALKING ABOUT?!
YOU RUINED MY SHOT, YOU BIG JERK!
NOW LEAVE ME ALONE!
SLASH!
IF THAT WAS REAL IT WOULD HAVE HURT!
I WAS SAVING THIS FOR A SPECIAL SOMEONE.
BUT I'M GOING TO ENJOY CORRUPTING YOUR HARD DRIVE!

BAM! BAM!
BAM! BAM!
BAM!
WHAT THE--?!
W-WHO'S THERE?
NIGEL PENHURST, FROM A.T.A.C.!

UM... NEVER HEARD OF IT.
YOU WOULDN'T HAVE. NOW OPEN THIS DOOR!
UM, OKAY...JUST A SECOND!

WHAM!
I'M AFRAID YOUR TIME IS UP, YOUNG LADY!
CONGRATULATIONS, GENTLEMEN...WE HAVE HER.
SHE WON'T BE DESTROYING ANYONE ELSE'S COMPUTERSFOR A VERY VERY LONG TIME!
ULP!

LOOK, FRANK--
SHE'S GONE!
I GUESS WE CAN GO NOW.
NIGEL LOGGED OFF HER COMPUTER. THE THREAT IS OVER.
I GUESS SO!
ONCE WE SHOW THESE BRIGANDS WHAT HARDYS ARE MADE OF!
THAT'S ANOTHER THING I LOVE ABOUT MY BROTHER.
HAVE AT THEE!
HE'S THE ONLY GUY I KNOW WHO CAN USE "BRIGAND" IN A SENTENCE AND MAKE IT SOUND COOL!

CHAPTER TWO:
"THE FINISHED LINE!"
I'M FRANK HARDY.
THAT'S ME, IN SECOND PLACE BEHIND MY BROTHER, JOE.
HE'S THINKS OF HIM-SELF AS THE ATHLETE OF THE FAMILY.
I DON'T DO ANYTHING TO DISSUADE HIM OF THAT NOTION.
THAT WAS CLOSE!
YOU'RE JUST TRYING TO BE NICE.
10

BAYPORT WINS AGAIN!
HARDYS ROCK!
YEAH, JOE!
YOU MADE US PROUD, BOYS...
...NOW HIT THE SHOWERS!
YES, SIR!

A LITTLE LOUDER, FRANK
I CAN'T HEAR YOU OVER THE ROAR OF THE CROWD.
HE'S JUST JOKING. THAT'S HIS SENSE OF HUMOR.
JOE IS ONE OF THE MOST MODEST DOWN-TO-EARTH GUYS I KNOW.
HE'S LIKE ANY OTHER YOUNGER BROTHER...HE ENJOYS GIVING HIS OLDER BROTHER GRIEF.
04

YOU KNOW YOU ALMOST HAD ME IN THAT LAST LAP.
REALLY? I HADN'T NOTICED.
04
10

A LITTLE LATER WE LEAVE FROM THE SIDE DOOR.
HE PRETENDS TO SOAK UP THE CHEERS, BUT HE'S ACTUALLY KIND OF SHY WHEN IT COMES TO ADULATION.
WHAT DO YOU SAY TO A PIZZA, FRANK?

I SAY "WINNER BUYS!"
HA! HOW YOU FIGURE? IT'S NOT LIKE THERE WAS ANY PRIZE MONEY FOR THAT RACE!

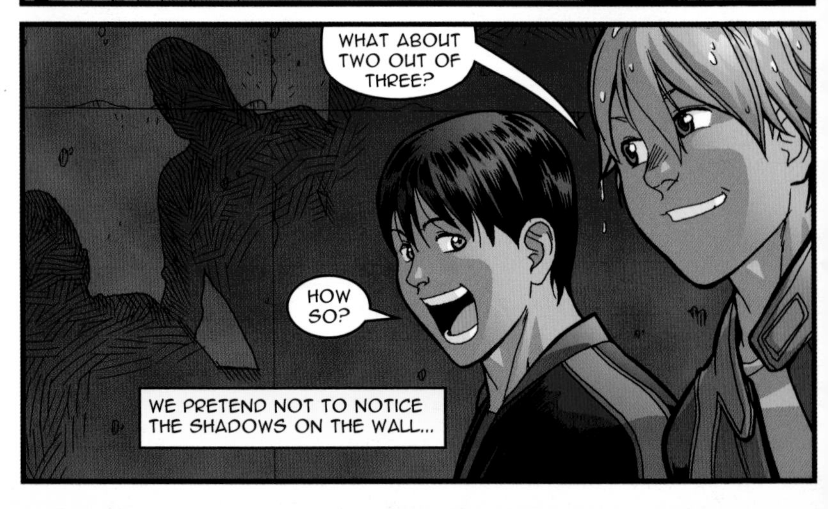
WHAT ABOUT TWO OUT OF THREE?
HOW SO?
WE PRETEND NOT TO NOTICE THE SHADOWS ON THE WALL...

CHAPTER THREE:
"WINNER TAKE FALL!"
WHOEVER TAKES DOWN THE MOST OF THESE SKI MASKED ASSAILANTS... BUYS DINNER!
THAT'S MY COMPETITIVE SPIRIT FOR YOU.
AND THAT'S MY BROTHER RISING TO THE OCCASION--
DEAL!
--EVEN IF IT MEANS GOING LOW!

ONE OF THE THINGS WE LEARNED--TAUGHT OURSELVES REALLY--
--LONG BEFORE A.T.A.C. TRAINED US--
HEY, DON'T GO TRASHIN' TRASH CANS!
HUNH?

--WAS TO MAKE THE MOST OF OUR ENVIRONMENT WHEN WE'RE IN A FIGHT.
SPLANG!
THE LIDS ARE VERY HANDY IN A FIGHT--
BOTH FOR DEFENSE AND FOR OFFENSE!
PLTANG!
URNGH!

ME? I'M GIVEN TO A WISECRACK ONCE AND A WHILE.
FRANK, LESS SO.
HE'S MORE CEREBRAL.
IT'S NOT ENOUGH TO DEFEAT AN OPPONENT, HE NEEDS TO STUDY THEM TOO.
THAT'S THE FOURTH ONE.
WERE YOU KEEPING TRACK?
LET'S ASK THEM...AND WHY THEY ATTACKED US.

WAIT!
STOP!
WE GIVE UP!
UNCLE!
WE'RE WITH A.T.A.C. SUPPORT!
WE WERE DISPATCHED TO BRING YOU TO HEADQUARTERS! OUR APOLOGIES FOR NOT IDENTIFYING OURSELVES SOONER.
A.T.A.C.
OH, SORRY.
HEH HEH.

A SURPRISE PARTY? FOR OUR DAD?
SO HE DOESN'T EVEN KNOW WE'RE COMING?

NOBODY DOES EXCEPT NIGEL AND THE FOUR OF US. DO YOU KNOW HOW HARD IT IS TO KEEP A SECRET IN A COMPLEX FILLED WITH SPIES?

I CAN IMAGINE.
YOU EVEN HAD TO BLIND-FOLD US SO WE WOULDN'T KNOW WHERE A.T.A.C. H.Q. IS.
WE APPRECIATE YOUR EXTRA CAUTION TO PROTECT ITS LOCATION.

ISN'T IT FUNNY HOW FAR WE'VE COME OVER THE YEARS?
FROM BOY DETECTIVES--
--TO UNDERCOVER BROTHERS.
IT WAS AN HONOR THAT DAD PICKED US AS THE FIRST TWO AGENTS RECRUITED.
WE'VE HAD QUITE A FEW ADVENTURES.
KIDS, HUH?
AND WHO CAN FORGET THE OCEAN OF OSYRIA?
IT SOUNDS LIKE WE'RE JUST RAMBLING...

BUT REALLY IT WAS JUST A COVER...
...WHILE WE CONCENTRATED ON THE CLUES AS TO OUR WHEREABOUTS.
AT FIFTY FIVE MILES AN HOUR HEADING NORTH BY NORTHEAST OUT OF BAYPORT...
WE CROSSED TWO SMALL BRIDGES AND CLIMBED AN ESTIMATED TEN THOUSAND FEET ABOVE SEA LEVEL...
GENTLEMEN, WE'RE HERE.
...UP MOUNTAIN ROADS AS WE COULD TELL FROM OUR EARS POPPING.

YOU CAN TAKE OFF YOUR BLIND-FOLDS.
JUST IN CASE, WE WEREN'T REALLY BEING TAKEN TO A.T.A.C.'S BASE.
YOU CAN NEVER BE TOO CAREFUL.

BUT THIS WAS DEFINITELY THE PLACE!

WOW! THIS PLACE IS AS COOL AS I ALWAYS THOUGHT IT WOULD BE!
I CAN'T THINK OF ANY-THING TO ADD TO THAT, EXCEPT...
MORE WOW.

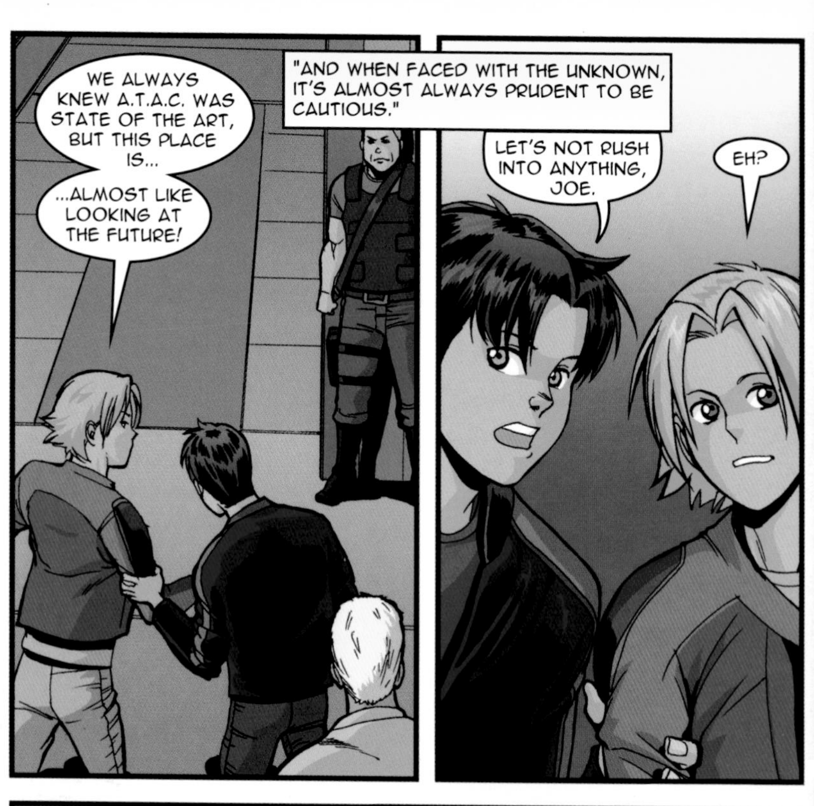
WE ALWAYS KNEW A.T.A.C. WAS STATE OF THE ART, BUT THIS PLACE IS...
...ALMOST LIKE LOOKING AT THE FUTURE!
"AND WHEN FACED WITH THE UNKNOWN, IT'S ALMOST ALWAYS PRUDENT TO BE CAUTIOUS."
LET'S NOT RUSH INTO ANYTHING, JOE.
EH?

THIS IS A HIGHLY PROTECTED COMPOUND...
WITH A VERY ELABORATE SECURITY SYSTEM, NO DOUBT.
WHOA, A LASER DEFENSE SYSTEM. I DIDN'T EVEN NOTICE IT.
FEW DO.
I'M IMPRESSED.

BUT THIS DEVICE DOES MUCH MORE THAN ALERT US TO TROUBLE.
ALLOW ME TO DEMON-STRATE:
A COIN.

FLIP
IP
IP
IP
IP
IP

ZAAAP!
THAT IS ONE POWERFUL LASER!
HOW--?!
MOTION DETECTORS.

HEY! IF FRANK HADN'T STOPPED ME--?!
AUTOMATED DEFENSES ARE IMPORTANT, SIR. BUT IF YOU BECOME TOO DEPENDENT ON IT--
WHATEV.
THE SECURITY SYSTEM HERE AT A.T.A.C. IS WITHOUT PEER, GENTLEMEN.

I'M JUST SAYING TECHNOLOGY CAN AUGMENT THE HUMAN EYE--
--BUT NOTHING REPLACES GOOD OLD-FASHIONED VIGILANCE.

PERHAPS YOU'RE RIGHT.
WELCOME TO A.T.A.C. HQ. THE SYSTEM HAS BEEN DEACTIVATED FOR THE MOMENT.
THANK YOU.
YEAH.
"THANKS."

ALL THIS FOR DAD?
THIS PLACE IS A BASKETBALL COURT. BUT FOR TODAY IT SERVES AS A BANQUET HALL.
WE'VE SPARED NO EXPENSE TO CELEBRATE YOUR DAD'S BIRTHDAY.
UM, YEAH, ABOUT THAT...?
OUR FATHER ISN'T REALLY ONE FOR BEING THE CENTER OF ATTENTION.
SIR, THE MASTER CHEF NEEDS TO SPEAK TO YOU.
HE SAYS IT'S A BIT OF AN EMERGENCY.

I'M ON IT!
GENTLEMEN, WE'VE TAKEN THE LIBERTY OF OBTAINING SUITS FOR YOU.
THANK YOU?

NOT THAT MUCH LATER...
THIS IS WHERE WE'RE SUPPOSED TO CHANGE OUR CLOTHES?
SPARED NO EXPENSE, HUH?

MORE LIKE THEY DIDN'T SPEND ANYTHING.
CREEEAK

I HOPE DAD APPRECIATES THIS.
HE WILL...IF ANYONE THINKS TO EVER LOOK FOR US BACK HERE.
HA HAH.

UNBELIEVABLE. MILLIONS OF DOLLARS POURED INTO THIS PLACE--
--AND I'M SURE IT WOULD FALL APART IN TWO MINUTES WITHOUT ME.

BUT I AM GOOD AT WHAT--
REX?
EH--?

FENTON!
YOU'RE NOT DUE FOR ANOTHER HOUR!
I WAS IN THE NEIGHBORHOOD. AND YOU LOOK BUSY--
--ANYTHING I CAN DO TO HELP OUT?

NO!
I MEAN, NO...NO, NOT AT ALL. NOTHING TO WORRY ABOUT.
JUST, UM, SOME, UM, TROUBLE IN, UM, THE KITCHEN.
NOTHING YOU NEED TO WORRY YOURSELF OVER!

I'M NOT WORRIED AT ALL. IT'S NOT AN IMPOSITION--WE'RE ALL ON THE SAME TEAM, REX.
AFTER YOU?
THIS IS ABSURD! I DID NOT ORDER A METRIC TON OF OLIVES!

I DID NOT ORDER ANY OLIVES AT ALL--LET ALONE A TON!
I'M ONLY DOING MY JOB, SIR. I WAS TOLD TO DROP THEM OFF HERE.

WHAT SEEMS TO BE THE TROUBLE, GENTLEMEN?
THE TROUBLE IS--THIS YOUNG MAN IS AN IDIOT!
WHOLESOME CATERERS
I CONFESS TO BEING A BIT CONFUSED BY ALL OF THIS.
WHY IS THERE A CHEF AND A CATERER ON THE GROUNDS?

LOOK, YOU JUST NEED TO INSPECT THE TRUCK TO MAKE SURE THE CARGO IS CORRECT.
THEN I'M SURE WE'LL ALL BE HAPPY.

WELL, OKAY...
MAYBE NOT ALL OF US.
SACRE...!
>ULP<

CHAPTER FOUR: "SURPRISE!"
MR. FENTON HARDY.
WE'VE MET YOUR SONS, OF COURSE.
IT'S SOMETHING OF AN HONOR TO MEET YOU. I'M NICOLINA AND THIS IS MY SISTER--
SHIRA, YES.
THE SISTERS NOIR. YOUR REPUTATION PRECEDES YOU.

YOU'LL EXCUSE ME IF I DON'T SHAKE HANDS?
HAVE TO REACH THE EMERGENCY SHUT-DOWN BUTTON...!
TRYING TO CLOSE DOWN THE ENTIRE COMPLEX?
KIK!
ARE YOU ARROGANT ENOUGH TO THINK WE HAVEN'T PLANNED EVERY DETAIL OF THIS OPERATION?
I ONLY KNOW JOE AND FRANK WERE NOT VERY IMPRESSED BY YOUR SKILLS.
WHA--?! THOSE TWO--
IGNORE HIM, SISTER. HE'S BAITING YOU.
SEE? I'M NOT LETTING HIM DISTRACT ME FROM DISABLING THE FAIL-SAFE SYSTEM.
CLICK!
THERE!

SOON...
THEY COULDN'T REMEMBER OUR SHOE SIZE?!
A.T.A.C. PROPER HAS MORE THINGS TO WORRY ABOUT THAN BUYING US SHOES.
WE'LL LOCATE AGENT REX AND HE'LL SORT IT OUT.
WHAT ARE YOU DOING THERE?
THERE'RE SECURITY CONSOLES THROUGH-OUT THE BUILDING.
IT SHOULD BE SIMPLE ENOUGH TO LOCATE ANYONE ON THE GROUNDS.
"SIMPLE," FRANK?
TAP TAP TIP TAP TAP TIP TIP TAPPITY TAP
SIMPLE ENOUGH.

"SEE? THE BASKETBALL COURT-TURNED-BALLROOM.
"THE GUESTS ARE JUST ARRIVING-- LIKE CLOCKWORK."

IS THAT THE GOVERNOR?
AND LOOK AT BROCKMAN-- THE GUY WHO TRAINS A LOT OF THE AGENTS IN HAND TO HAND COMBAT.
COULD HE LOOK ANY LESS COMFORTABLE?

BRAKABRAKABRAKA!
THAT SOUND--?!
GUNFIRE!

LADIES AND GENTLEMEN AND ESTEEMED GUESTS!
WELCOME TO THE BIRTHDAY FESTIVITIES FOR MR. FENTON HARDY!
SINCE YOU WERE ALL FORCED TO LEAVE ANY ARMAMENTS AT THE DOOR--
--I'M SURE IT GOES WITHOUT SAYING THAT ANYONE WHO DOESN'T FOLLOW OUR EXPLICIT DIRECTIONS GETS NO BIRTHDAY CAKE.

DID THEY JUST--?!
BREACH ONE OF THE MOST FORTIFIED BUILDINGS IN THE WORLD?
YES.
FOR THE REST OF YOUR VERY SHORT LIVES.

COME ON! WE'VE GOT TO FREE DAD AND THE OTHERS!
WE WILL! BUT FOR THE SECOND TIME TONIGHT--
--YOU NEED TO THINK THIS THROUGH BEFORE YOU RUSH INTO ACTION!
WE DON'T KNOW HOW MANY PEOPLE THE NOIRS BROUGHT WITH THEM.
THEY MUST HAVE PEOPLE LOOKING FOR STRAGGLERS.
SO WE HAVE TO BE SOMEWHERE ELSE--*NOW!*
YOU'RE RIGHT. AGAIN.

WHAT A WASTE OF TIME.
RIGHT? EVERY-ONE WHO IS HERE WAS ALREADY AT THE PARTY.

SEE? WHY DO WE ALWAYS GET THE STUPID ASSIGNMENTS?
MAYBE BECAUSE YOU KEEP ASKING SHIRA FOR HER PHONE NUMBER?

PLEASE. SHE DIGS ME.
DIGS YOU A GRAVE IS MORE LIKE IT.
THIS HALLWAY IS CLEAR. SURPRISE, NOT.

LET'S GET BACK TO THE PARTY.
FINE.

PHEW!
THAT EXPRESSION ON JOE'S FACE--?
SOMETHING'S WRONG?!

HE LET GO--HE'S FALLING!
BUT WHY?

NOW!
NO WAY HE'S GETTING THE DROP ON--!
WAY.
KICK!
KLACK!
I HAVE THEIR WEAPONS COVERED!
BUT BEING OUT COLD AND ALL, I DON'T THINK THEY'LL BE NEEDING THEM ANY WAY.

I HAVE TO ASK, JOE.
HOW DID YOU KNOW THEY SAW US?

THEY DIDN'T.
I NOTICED OUR FOOTPRINTS IN THE DUST.
YOU KNEW IT WAS ONLY ANOTHER MOMENT BEFORE THEY WOULD LOOK UP.
THAT WAS EXCELLENT.

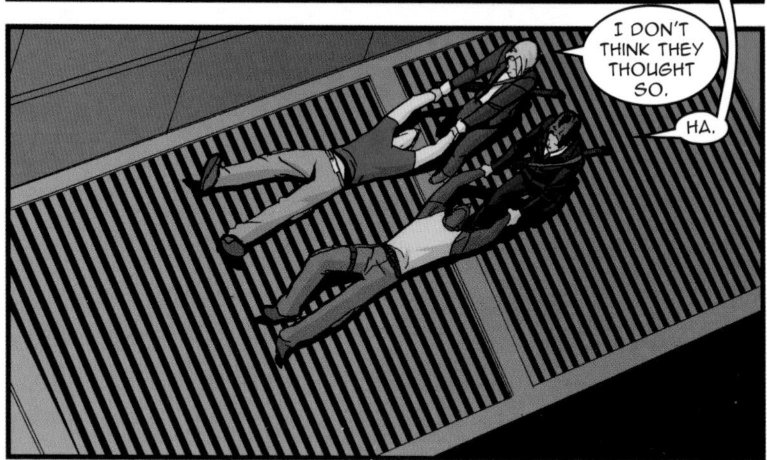
I DON'T THINK THEY THOUGHT SO.
HA.

THERE'S A REASON YOU'RE RUMMAGING THROUGH THAT UTILITY CLOSET.
YES.
DOES IT HAVE ANYTHING TO DO WITH THE FACT--
--WE CAN'T GET INTO A FIRE FIGHT WITH THE NOIRS AND THEIR TERRORIST FRIENDS WITHOUT ENDANGERING LIVES?

YES.
IF WE'RE GOING TO TAKE THIS PLACE BACK IN THE NAME OF A.T.A.C.--
--WE'RE GOING TO HAVE TO GET CREATIVE.
ROPE AND A CHAIR.
A REGULAR GOLDMINE YOU HAVE THERE, FRANK.

MY SISTER AND I APOLOGIZE FOR PUTTING A DAMPER ON THE FESTIVITIES.
OUR FAMILY HAS SOME UNFINISHED BUSINESS WITH THE HARDYS.
"JIMMY AND ROSE SANTORA.
"WORTH NEARLY TEN MILLION EACH!
"DR. MASON FRYES. THE WORLD'S MOST TALENTED CODE BREAKER.
"THE C.I.A. WILL PAY MILLIONS TO GET YOU BACK ALIVE.

BUT YOU CAN'T REALLY BLAME US FOR TAKING ADVANTAGE OF THIS GUEST LIST.
THE BIGGEST MOVERS, SHAKERS AND HOSTAGES ALL IN ONE ROOM!
"KING NUBARI.
"WHAT IS A KINGDOM WITHOUT ITS KING?"
REST ASSURED. WE HAVE THOUGHT OF EVERY--
IIIIIIIIEEEEEEE!!!!

REET REET REET REET

REEEEE EET

THUMP
HO HO HO
NOW I HAVE
THE WEAPONS
"HO HO HO.
NOW I HAVE THE
WEAPONS."

IIIIIIIIIIIIIIIIEEEEEE!
THE BOYS.
THEY'RE HERE. THEY'RE SAFE.
HOW CAN YOU TELL?

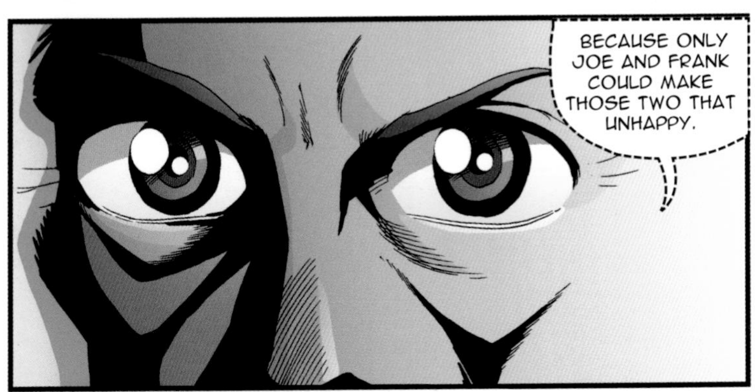
BECAUSE ONLY JOE AND FRANK COULD MAKE THOSE TWO THAT UNHAPPY.

"HO HO HO?"
I SAW IT IN A MOVIE. LET'S GO.

DO YOU THINK THAT WAS IT? ALL THE TERRORISTS IN ONE ROOM?
I THINK THAT WAS MOST OF THEM. MAYBE SOME POSTED AT THE MAIN DOORS.
BUT THE CLOSER THEY KEEP THE HOSTAGES...
...THE EASIER THEY ARE TO CONTROL?

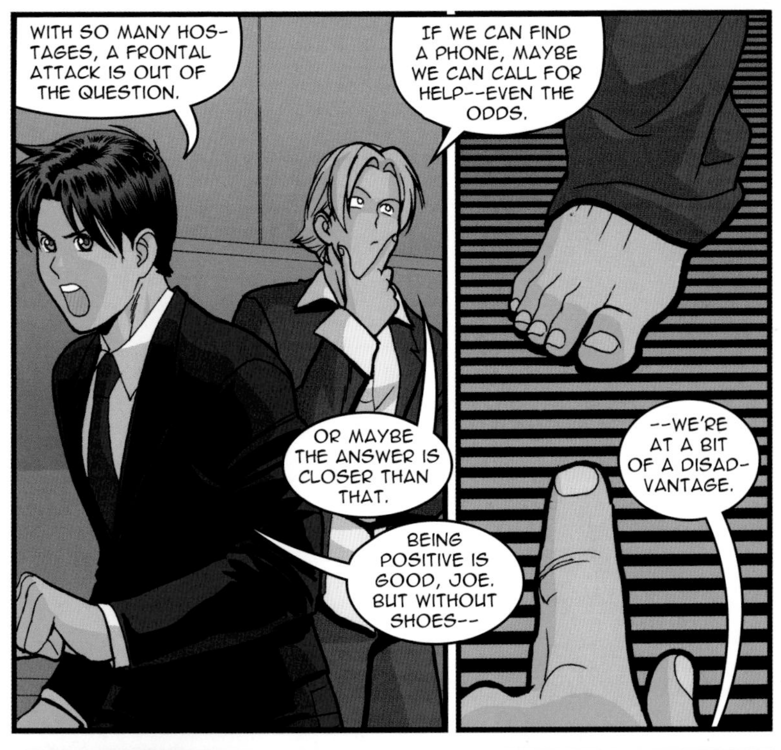
WITH SO MANY HOSTAGES, A FRONTAL ATTACK IS OUT OF THE QUESTION.
IF WE CAN FIND A PHONE, MAYBE WE CAN CALL FOR HELP--EVEN THE ODDS.
OR MAYBE THE ANSWER IS CLOSER THAN THAT.
BEING POSITIVE IS GOOD, JOE. BUT WITHOUT SHOES--
--WE'RE AT A BIT OF A DISADVANTAGE.

I SEE THAT, BUT I HAVE AN IDEA.
BACK ME UP?
YOU HAVE TO ASK?

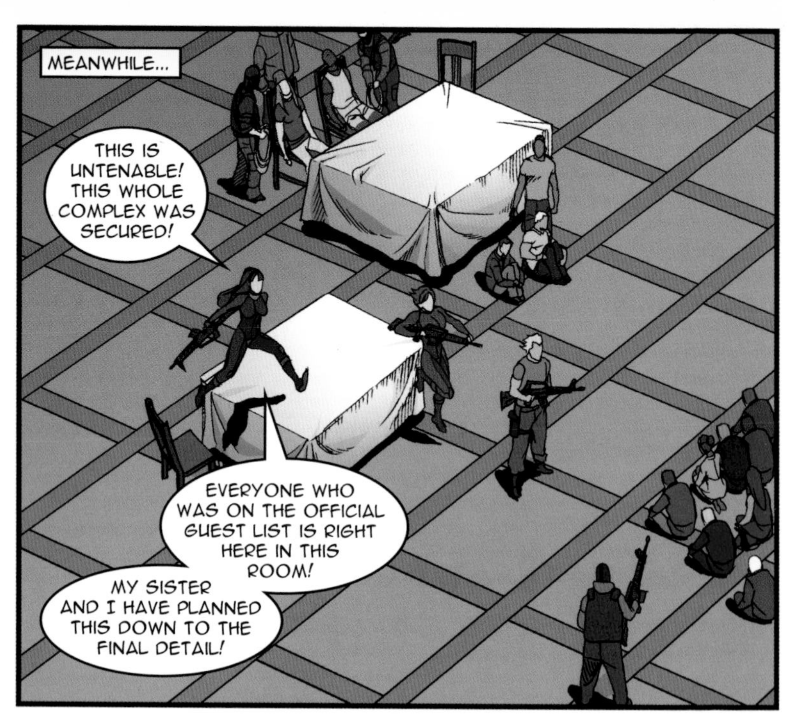
MEANWHILE...
THIS IS UNTENABLE! THIS WHOLE COMPLEX WAS SECURED!
EVERYONE WHO WAS ON THE OFFICIAL GUEST LIST IS RIGHT HERE IN THIS ROOM!
MY SISTER AND I HAVE PLANNED THIS DOWN TO THE FINAL DETAIL!

WHICH MEANS IF THIS OPERATION FAILS--IT IS YOUR FAULT! GOT IT?!
NOW GO FIND THAT INTRUDER!
NICOLINA IS IN HIGH DUNGEON. BUT SHIRA SEEMS A LITTLE.... DISTRACTED.
HMMM.

GOSH! I HOPE NOBODY FINDS ME.
HERE ALL ALONE. BY MYSELF.
WITH NO WEAPONS.

LOOK--IT'S A KID!
STOP RIGHT THERE, KID!
OH, NO.

SHOULD WE SHOOT HIM?!
NOT UNLESS WE HAVE--WAIT, HE'S STOPPING!
YOU DON'T MISS A THING!
SKIIIIIID!

CHAPTER FIVE:
"COPS AND ROBBERS"
EXCEPT FOR THE LASER-POWERED SECURITY SYSTEM I CONVINCED MY BROTHER TO JURY RIG BACK TOGETHER!
YOU'RE PLAN WORKED PERFECTLY, JOE! YOU LEAD THEM RIGHT HERE!
WHAT THE--?!
OUR GUNS! THEY'RE RUINED!

MINE IS FINE. SEE?
LET'S TURN THIS THING OFF BEFORE SOME-ONE LOSES A FINGER.
NOW, GENTLEMEN-- YOUR HANDS WHERE I CAN SEE THEM.

I KNEW WE SHOULD HAVE SHOT HIM.
SHUT-UP, HANK.

WOULD YOU MIND TERRIBLY IF I BORROW YOUR CELL PHONE? I NEED TO MAKE A CALL.
YEAH, SURE.
THANK YOU.

THAT'S MY BROTHER FOR YOU. HE HAS THE POLITE GENE.
IT'S RINGING.
SHERIFF'S OFFICE.
SHERIFF COLLIG, YOU'RE THERE!

FRANK HARDY? SORRY I COULDN'T MAKE YOUR FATHER'S SURPRISE PARTY TONIGHT.
I'VE BEEN AT WORK THIS WHOLE--
I'M SORRY TO SAY, THIS IS ABOUT WORK.

OUR FATHER'S IN A DANGEROUS SITUATION AND WE NEED YOUR HELP!
DOZENS OF LIVES ARE AT STAKE.
OF COURSE, I'LL BE RIGHT THERE!

HANK?! ARE YOU THERE?!
UNBELIEVABLE! HAVE WE LOST TWO MORE MEN?!
WHO IS THIS INTRUDER?!

ONCE HE SECURES HIMSELF IN THE LAB, THERE'LL BE NO STOPPING HIM-- WHOEVER HE IS.

YOU'RE EXACTLY RIGHT, MR. HARDY!
MY SISTER AND I WILL GUARD MR. HARDY AND HIS GUESTS!
THE REST OF YOU TO THE LAB-- GO!
PERHAPS I SHOULDN'T HAVE SAID ANYTHING.

THE LAB.
SO THIS IS THE PLACE THE EGGHEADS MAKE ALL THE GADGETS WE USE ON OUR CASES?
THE VERY SAME. NOW IF WE COULD FIND SOMETHING HERE TO EVEN THE ODDS BEFORE--
THERE YOU ARE! HEY, THEY'RE KIDS!
PUT YOUR HANDS UP--NOW!
?!
KLIK!
RIGHT AWAY, SIR!
ARMS UP, JOE--WE DON'T WANT ANY TROUBLE.

WHAT THE HECK--?!
IT'S LIKE SOMETHING IS...PULLING ON OUR GUNS?!
MORE LIKE YANKING?!
I CAN'T HOLD ON!
ME NEITHER--LIKE THEY'RE MAGNETIZED!
EXACTLY!
THAT'S WHAT HAPPENS WHEN YOU ATTACK A SECRET AGENT IN A LAB WITH HIGH TECH PROTO-TYPES.
KLAK!
LIKE THIS ONE!

CHAPTER SIX:
"ZAPPED!"
IT IS A LOCALIZED PACIFICATION FIELD-- BUILT RIGHT INTO THE FLOOR TILES.
GOOD THING IT KNOCKS YOU OUT COLD BEFORE IT ACTUALLY HURTS, HUH?
HELLO?

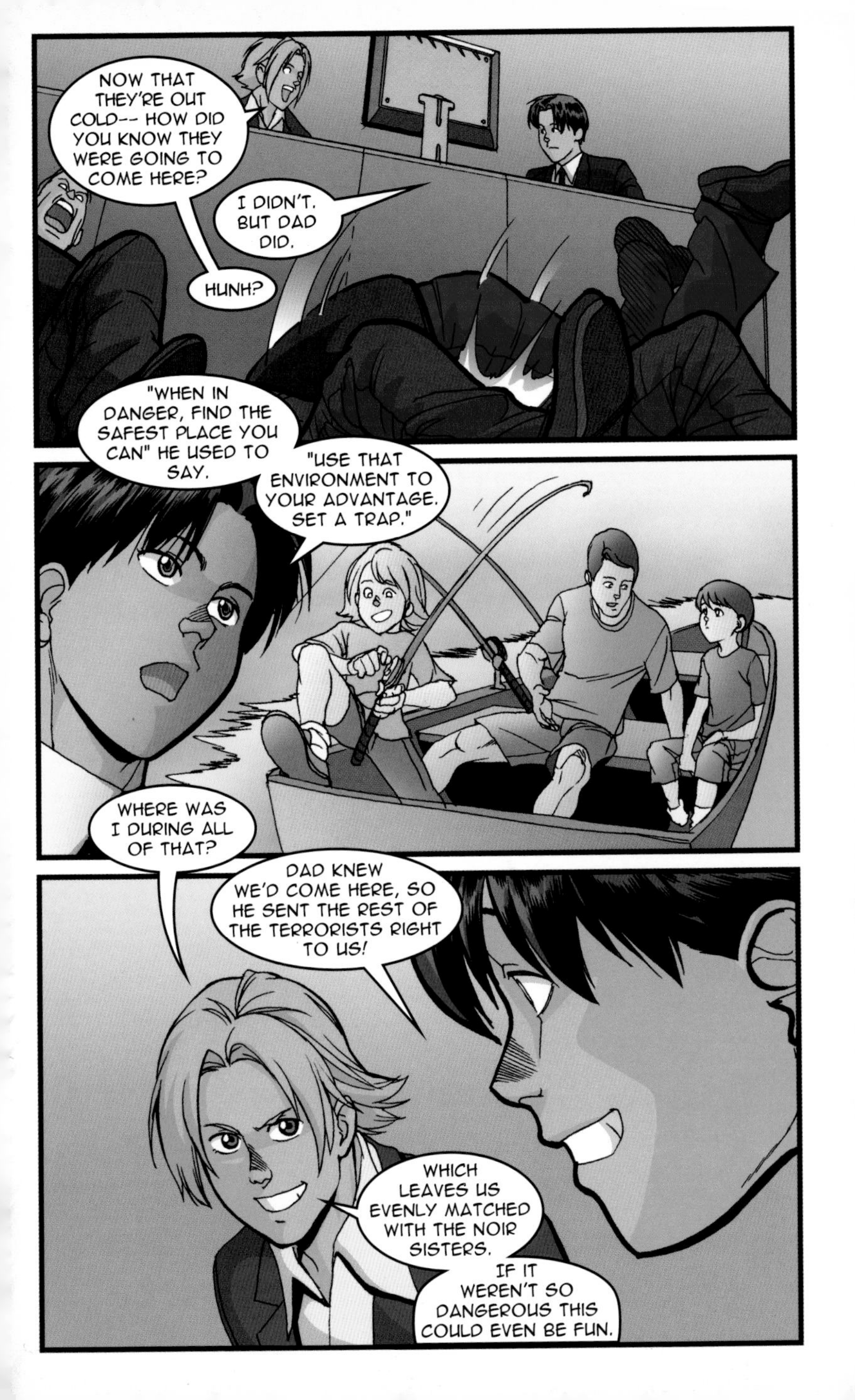
NOW THAT THEY'RE OUT COLD-- HOW DID YOU KNOW THEY WERE GOING TO COME HERE?
I DIDN'T. BUT DAD DID.
HUNH?
"WHEN IN DANGER, FIND THE SAFEST PLACE YOU CAN" HE USED TO SAY.
"USE THAT ENVIRONMENT TO YOUR ADVANTAGE. SET A TRAP."
WHERE WAS I DURING ALL OF THAT?
DAD KNEW WE'D COME HERE, SO HE SENT THE REST OF THE TERRORISTS RIGHT TO US!
WHICH LEAVES US EVENLY MATCHED WITH THE NOIR SISTERS.
IF IT WEREN'T SO DANGEROUS THIS COULD EVEN BE FUN.

FENTON. WHAT ARE YOU--?

STOP RIGHT THERE.
I'VE STOPPED, NICOLINA.
NOW... ISN'T IT YOUR TURN?
WH-WHAT ARE YOU TALK-ING ABOUT?

I MET YOUR FATHER. I KNOW HE'S A CRUEL MAN.
HE'S A FIGHTER, AND HE'LL DO ANY-THING TO WIN.
BUT THAT'S NOT WHO YOU ARE ...IS IT?
YOU'RE MORE THAN THAT... AREN'T YOU?

HAND ME YOUR GUN, NICOLINA.
YOU CAN STOP ALL THIS.

WHAM!
URGHN!
TRYING TO TURN MY OWN SISTER ON ME?!
ALL YOU HARDYS ARE THE SAME!
BUT YOUR SISTER IS DIFFERENT THAN YOUR FATHER AND YOU. THAT WAS MY POINT.
SHIRA, PLEASE!
BE QUIET! I'M GOING TO END THIS!
IF YOU DO...

... WHO IS GOING TO BLOW OUT MY CANDLES?
HIS BIRTHDAY CAKE?! BUT HOW DID IT GET IN HERE?

NOT ON ITS OWN--THAT'S FOR SURE!
FATHER MENTIONED THEY PULLED A TRICK LIKE THIS AT THE HOTEL.
NICOLINA--PULL BACK THE APRON, I'LL COVER YOU.
Y-YES, SHIRA.

HMP. USUALLY THIS TRICK WORKS.
I GUESS WE WERE OUT-SMARTED THIS TIME.

CHAPTER SEVEN: "MAKE A WISH..."
JOE! FRANK! WHAT A PLEASANT SURPRISE!
SORRY, DAD. I GUESS WE FAILED YOU.
AT LEAST WE'LL BE TOGETHER IN THE END.
>SIGH<

THE END OF THE HARDYS. NOW THAT IS SOMETHING I'LL CELEBRATE!

ALLOW ME!

DON'T BOTHER MAKING A WISH, MR. HARDY! BECAUSE IN A MINUTE YOU'LL BE TOO DEAD TO ENJOY IT!

WHUMP!
SHIRA?!
WHAT HAPPENED... TO...
THE... CANDLES... TRICK...
... RELEASED... KNOCK OUT... GAS?

IT'S OKAY, NICOLINA.
YOU CAN REST NOW, YOUNG LADY. EVERYTHING IS OKAY.
IT'S ALL OVER...AND I PROMISE WHEN YOU WAKE UP--
--I'LL SEE THAT YOU BOTH GET ALL THE HELP YOU NEED TO BREAK YOURSELF FROM YOUR FATHER'S GRIP ON YOU.

THOSE KNOCK OUT CANDLES WE FOUND IN THE LAB WERE PERFECT.

WE WERE ABLE TO END THIS ALL WITHOUT ANYONE GETTING--

SLAM!
EVERYONE FREEZE!
--HURT?

GREAT, YOU ALL LOOK FINE!
WHAT HAPPENED TO THOSE TERRORISTS YOU MENTIONED ON THE PHONE?
THE REST OF THEM ARE TIED UP IN THE LAB, SHERIFF COLLIG.
BUT THANKS FOR COMING SO QUICKLY!
WITH THAT OUT OF THE WAY, MAYBE WE CAN GET BACK TO THE REASON WE ALL GATHERED HERE TODAY?
WHAT? I HAVEN'T HAD ENOUGH SURPRISES FOR ONE DAY, NIGEL?

LADIES AND GENTLEMAN, IT HAS BEEN FUN. AND I'M HONORED YOU ALL CAME TONIGHT.
BUT PERHAPS WE CAN CELEBRATE TOGETHER AT A LESS HECTIC TIME?

THE CAKE CAN WAIT, BOYS.
LET'S GO HOME.

I CAN THINK OF WORSE WAYS TO SPEND A BIRTHDAY.

LATER THAT NIGHT....
ALL THE LIGHTS ARE OUT.
MOM AND AUNT TRUDY MUST BE ASLEEP ALREADY.
JUST AS WELL. AFTER EVERYTHING WE'VE BEEN THROUGH--
--AN EARLY NIGHT WOULD BE PERFECT.

I AGREE.
I'M BEAT.

LET'S KEEP IT QUIET WHILE WE MAKE OURSELVES SOMETHING TO EAT.
WE DON'T WANT TO WAKE ANY-ONE.

CHAPTER EIGHT: "NO PLACE LIKE HOME"
SURPRISE!
PRICELESS!
HE DIDN'T SUSPECT A THING!
DID YOU SEE HIS FACE?

FOR ME?
YOU SHOULDN'T HAVE.
HA HA
TOO FUNNY.

REALLY, FENTON--DID YOU THINK YOU WERE GOING TO GET AWAY WITHOUT A PARTY?
NOW COME BLOW OUT YOUR CANDLES AND MAKE A WISH.
THANKFULLY, THERE'S ONLY TWO CANDLES!

DID YOU MAKE A WISH, DAD?
NO NEED TO, FRANK.

"I'VE ALREADY GOT THE GREATEST FAMILY A GUY COULD EVER WISH FOR."

THE END

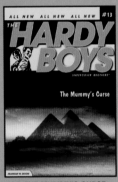

pecial Preview of THE HARDY BOYS Graphic Novel #16- "Shhhhhh!"
CHAPTER ONE: "THE GREAT BREAK OUT"
THERE YOU GO, HARDY--
--TRY TO MAKE THE SHOT NOW!
THBUMP!
I'M SORRY, SIR. DID YOU SAY SOMETHING...?

"THAT'S MY BROTHER, JOE HARDY.
"HE'S MAYBE THE BEST ATHLETE I KNOW.
"IT HAS ALLOWED US TO WORK UNDERCOVER DURING A NUMBER OF CASES FOR A.T.A.C.*"
"LIKE THIS ONE, HERE IN A FEDERAL PRISON.
*A.T.A.C.: AMERICAN TEENS AGAINST CRIME.

...I'M KIND OF BUSY RIGHT THIS MOMENT.
GRRRR.

YOU'VE GOT A SMART MOUTH, PUNK.
BUT I HAVE TO ADMIT, YOU'RE A HECK OF A PLAYER.
THANK YOU.
BUT...
...NOW I AM KIND OF DISTRACTED. BY THAT GYM BAG ON THE HIGH SCHOOL TEAM'S BENCH.
AND I'M NOT THE ONLY ONE INTERESTED IN IT, APPARENTLY.
Don't miss THE HARDY BOYS Graphic Novel # 16 – "Shhhhhh!"

WATCH OUT FOR PAPERCUTZ™

Welcome to a scary edition of the Papercutz Backpages, the place to find out all the latest news about the graphic novel publishers of THE HARDY BOYS, NANCY DREW, TALES FROM THE CRYPT, BIONICLE, and CLASSICS ILLUSTRATED. I'm Jim Salicrup, your Editor-in-Chief, and prime Papercutz promoter! We've got lots to talk about, so let's get right to it...

Things have taken a scary turn here at Papercutz! Don't panic -- we're not talking about any of our graphic novels suddenly vanishing from bookstore shelves! We're not talking that kind of scary! Thanks to your continued support, our sales are stronger than ever, and if any of our titles have vanished off the shelves, it's only because they are temporarily sold out! No, we're talking TALES FROM THE CRYPT scary — and how it's suddenly seeming to take over the pages of CLASSICS ILLUSTRATED and CLASSICS ILLUSTRATED DELUXE!

CLASSICS ILLUSTRATED #4 features world-famous cartoonist Gahan Wilson's creepy cartoons illustrated Edgar Allan Poe's "The Raven and Other Poems." And if that wasn't scary enough, CLASSICS ILLUSTRATED DELUXE #3 features an all-new adaptation by Marion Mousse of Mary Shelly's monster-masterwork "Frankenstein"!

Why have our CLASSICS ILLUSTRATED titles turned into a virtual vault of horror? The answer is obvious! After all, what is a "classic" if not a story so powerfully compelling that it leads to countless retellings? But we suspect that you've never experienced Poe's poems as seen through macabre cartoonist Gahan Wilson's bloodshot eyes, or the tale of Victor Frankenstein and his monster as dramatically brought to life, so to speak, by the dark visions of Marion Mousse.

Despite how many times the Frankenstein story has been told, it's as thought-provoking and as frightening now as the day it was when originally published in 1818. If you've never read the original novel you may be surprised that it's not the over-the-top crazy story so many adaptations may imply, but rather it's a serious tale tackling many major issues. Mousse takes great pains to restore many of Victor Frankenstein's motivations that lead to his "mad quest" to solve the ultimate mystery of life and death (as opposed to simply creating a monster).

In the pages that follow you'll see for yourself, the skill and artistry that Mousse brings to faithfully adapting this terrifying classic. Keep in mind, that the pages of CLASSICS ILLUSTRATED DELUXE are much larger than these pages, so to truly savor these pages, and to avoid eye-strain, be sure to pick up CLASSICS ILLUSTRATED DELUXE #3!

Thanks,

Jim

Caricature by Rick Parker

FULL-COLOR GRAPHIC NOVEL ADAPTATION
CLASSICS Illustrated®
Deluxe
FRANKENSTEIN
By Mary Shelley
Adapted by Marion Mousse
PAPERCUTZ

FOR MORE THAN A YEAR, I STUDIED ALL THE FORMS AND CONSE-QUENCES OF DEATH: THE FLESH DECOMPOSING, SLOWLY ROTTING...

...THE MATTER OF WHICH WE'RE ALL MADE, DEGRADING AND WASTING AWAY BEFORE VANISHING AS THOUGH THROUGH MAGIC.

FRANKENSTEIN...
...OUR LOCAL CELEBRITY HARD AT WORK.
...

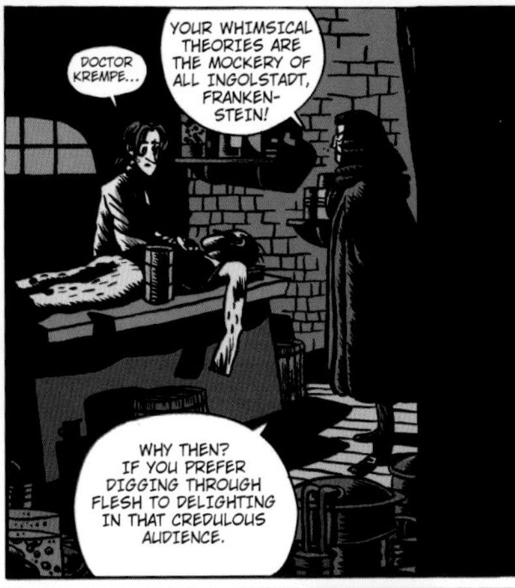
DOCTOR KREMPE...
YOUR WHIMSICAL THEORIES ARE THE MOCKERY OF ALL INGOLSTADT, FRANKEN-STEIN!
WHY THEN? IF YOU PREFER DIGGING THROUGH FLESH TO DELIGHTING IN THAT CREDULOUS AUDIENCE.

STILL CHASING AFTER YOUR MAD HEROES?! CORNELIUS AGRIPPA, PARACELSUS...
DON'T TELL ME THAT YOU'RE STILL A DISCIPLE OF THOSE COOKED-UP ABSURDITIES?!

PHILLIPUS AUREOLUS VON HOHENHEIM, KNOWN AS PARACELSUS, EMINENT ALCHEMIST, WHO CLAIMED TO HAVE EXPERIMENTED ON THE FAMOUS ELIXIR OF ETERNAL YOUTH AND CREATED...

...THE HOMUNCU-LUS, A SMALL LIVING BEING IN THE FORM OF A HUMAN!
I KNOW ALL THAT, FRANKENSTEIN!
SO YOU CONTINUE AND CONTINUE TO PERSIST! YOU PERSIST IN RIDICULING YOUR PROFESSORS, IN DISCREDITING OUR HONORABLE INSTITUTION?!!

WELL THEN! SO, I HEREAFTER FORBID YOU TO USE COURSE MATERIAL SUCH AS HUMAN REMAINS OUTSIDE OF YOUR COURSES!
UNTIL NOW, I'D MADE NO ASSUMPTIONS ABOUT YOUR CHARACTER, YOUNG MAN.

YES, I WAS HESITATING...I WAS HESITATING BETWEEN A YAHOO AND AN ENLIGHT-ENED SCIENTIST... NOW I KNOW.

A YAHOO!!
DO YOU HEAR, THEODORE?!
THAT OLD, PRETENTIOUS, BACKWARDS IMBECILE TREATED ME...
STOP...
VICTOR, STOP, I BEG YOU.
THEO...
YOU CAN'T, YOU HEAR, VICTOR? YOU CAN'T!
CHOOSING TO DISSECT A CORPSE, AGAINST THE SACROSANCT PRINCIPLE OF UNITY THAT UNDERLIES THE NOTION OF THE INDIVIDUAL, IS ALREADY A BLASPHEMY ACCORDING TO THE COMMITTEE!
BUT CLAIMING TO RECREATE THAT UNITY AND GIVING LIFE BACK TO IT...
... IT'S PURE FOLLY!!
THERE'S AN ESSENTIAL FACT, MY GOOD THEO, TRANSCENDING THE TRANSCENDENTAL!
AH! VICTOR...
THEO...
THEO, WHAT YOU'RE TALKING ABOUT IS RIDICULOUS! YOU'RE NOT EVEN A BELIEVER!
I DON'T RECOGNIZE YOU.
ME EITHER, VICTOR, ME EITHER.
ANYWAYS, DON'T WORRY, THE LABORATORIES ARE NOW CLOSED TO ME, I NO LONGER HAVE...
....ANY VICTIMS UPON WHOM TO PERPETRATE MY CRIMES! SO BE GLAD!!
I'VE LEFT SEVERAL BOOKS FOR YOU ON THE COUNTER... FROM DOCTOR WALDMAN.

THIS WAY, YOUNG MAN.

...
THE KEY...

AH, THE KEY TO PARADISE! CHOLERA, TYPHUS, COAL, ETC, A GIFT FROM HEAVEN FOR VAMPIRES.

SLOWLY, I CUT MYSELF OFF FROM EVERYONE AND INVITED MYSELF INTO THAT OTHER WORLD I WOULD NO LONGER LEAVE BEHIND.

HE SEEMS RATHER YOUNG TO BE UNDERTAKING THIS SORT OF THING.

THAT'S WHERE HE'LL SUCCEED OR FAIL. HE MUST TRY. OTHERWISE, HE'LL END UP BEING CONSUMED BY FEAR AND REGRET.
IT'S NOW OR NEVER.

HE'S GIFTED, MARKUS...MAYBE TOO MUCH SO.

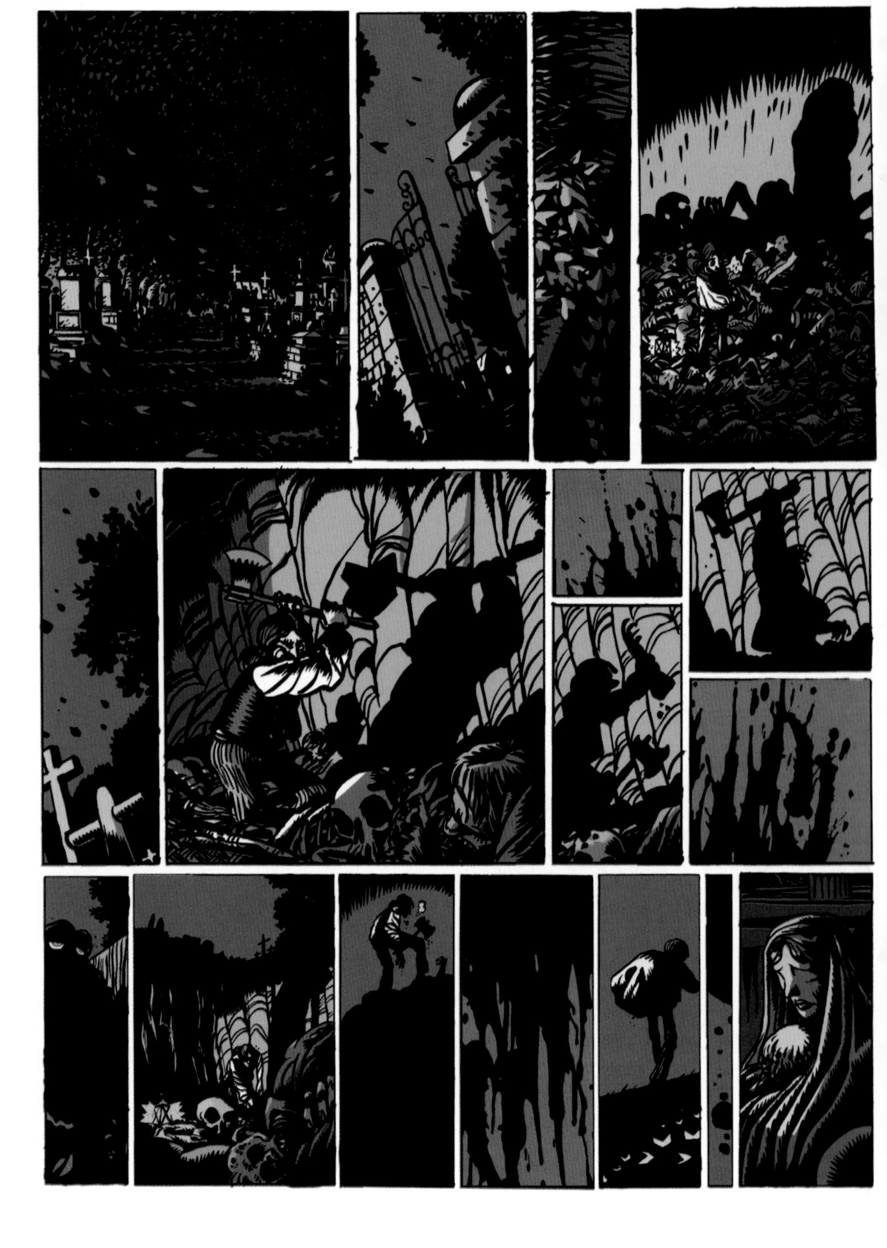

WINTER, SPRING, AND SUMMER PASSED AWAY DURING MY LABORS; BUT I DID NOT WATCH THE BLOSSOM OR THE EXPANDING LEAVES-SIGHTS WHICH BEFORE ALWAYS YIELDED ME SUPREME DELIGHT.

WAS EXHAUSTING MYSELF OVER ROTTING FLESH. MY NIGHTMARES TEMPERING MY ENTHUSIASM, ONLY THE ENERGY RESULTING FROM MY RESOLVE SUSTAINED ME.

I WAS MAKING PROGRESS, BUT WITH AN ANXIETY GROWING IN MEASURE WITH MY DISCOVERIES. I WAS SLOWLY EXTINGUISHING MYSELF, WHILE SEARCHING FOR THE MIRACULOUS SPARK.

RELENTLESSLY ON THE HUNT FOR THIS SPARK, I SCANNED THE HEAVENS AND BEGGED THEM TO BURST FORTH IN STORM. HOW IRONIC, NO? I WAS HOPING FOR RESURRECTION FROM THE SKY.

ELIZABETH, IT'S ME.
HENRY...
ELIZABETH, YOU'RE SO PALE. ALAS, I CAN GUESS WHY.
NONE...NO NEWS, HENRY, FOR ALMOST TEN DAYS!!

I ONLY WENT OUT AT NIGHT... I NO LONGER KEPT MY CORRESPONDENCE, I'D QUIETLY DISAPPEARED...WITHOUT BUDGING FROM MY LABORATORY, I'D STILL DISAPPEARED.
VICTOR! VICTOR!
OPEN UP!! IT'S ME, THEODORE. I BEG YOU, OPEN UP!!

IT'S NO USE.
I'VE NOT SEEN HIM IN TWO DAYS. HE'S NOT EVEN TOUCHING HIS MEALS...YET HE IS THERE. I HEAR HIM COMING AND GOING DAY AND NIGHT.

VICTOR! VICTOR!!

?!

WE'RE FINALLY THERE...
AT LAST!!
SOON YOU WILL HEAR THE WRATH OF HEAVEN!!

ITS WRATH WON'T BE IN VAIN TONIGHT!!
CURSED HEAVEN, THUNDER ON!!

IT'S UNFORTUNATE THAT YOU CANNOT WITNESS THE GLORY OF YOUR OWN CREATOR.
HOW HE COMMANDED NATURE TO GIVE YOU LIFE!!

TALES FROM THE CRYPT FANS!

ALL-NEW STORIES! FULL-COLOR GRAPHIC NOVEL!
TERROR
TALES FROM THE CRYPT
FEATURING...
THE CRYPT-KEEPER
THE OLD WITCH
THE VAULT-KEEPER
ALL-NEW STORIES! FULL-COLOR GRAPHIC NOVEL!
NO. 4
CRYPT-KEEPING IT REAL
TERROR
TALES FROM THE CRYPT
FEATURING 2 ALL-NEW STORIES BY JOE R. LANSDALE & JOHN L. LANSDALE TODAY'S TOP HORROR WRITERS!
FEATURING...
THE CRYPT-KEEPER
THE OLD WITCH
THE VAULT-KEEPER
PAPERCUTZ